11200

RACHEL ISADORA

My Ballet Class

Wizard's Wardrobe

Greenwillow Books, New York

Published by Greenwillow Books
A Division of William Morrow
& Company, Inc.,
105 Madison Avenue,
New York, N.Y. 10016

Printed in the United
States of America
First Edition

10   9   8   7   6   5   4   3   2   1

Library of Congress
Cataloging in Publication Data
Isadora, Rachel.
My ballet class.
Summary: A young girl describes her
ballet class which meets twice a week.
[1.   Ballet dancing—Fiction]
I.   Title.   PZ7.I793My   [E]
79-16297   ISBN 0-688-80253-2
ISBN 0-688-84253-4 lib. bdg.

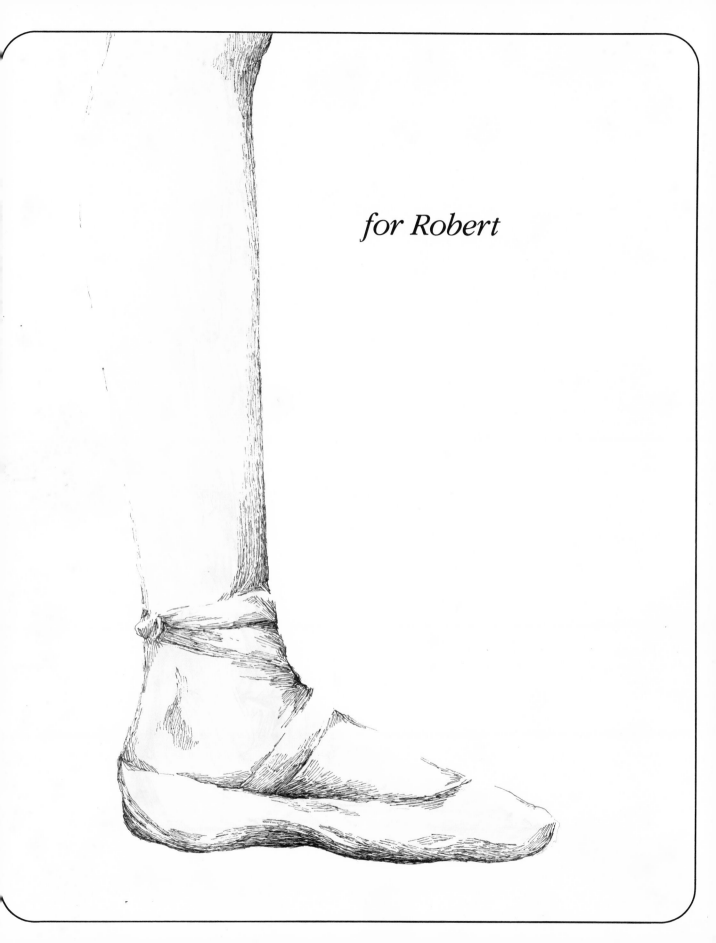

for Robert

Today is my ballet class.
I go twice a week.

I change my clothes
in the girls' dressing room.
I put on my tights
and leotard.

I tie the ribbons of my ballet slippers around my ankles.

I put my braids up into buns.
My friend Madeleine waits for me.

My ballet class is in a big studio.
I say "hello" to my friends.

Madam plays the piano for my class.
My favorite music is from <u>Swan Lake</u>.

Mr. Lucien is the teacher.
The first step we do is at the barre.
He shows us how to plié.
Then we do it.

We dance many steps.
We stand up on our toes
in relevé.

We do a passé. Mr. Lucien corrects me.

We do an arabesque.

The hardest step for me is developpé à la seconde. I must hold my leg up high for a long time.

Then we leave the barre.
We copy Mr. Lucien and do
the five classical positions.

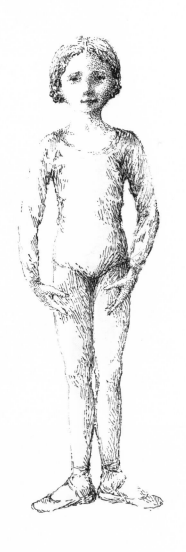

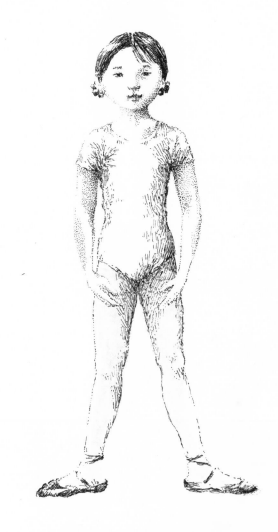

first

second

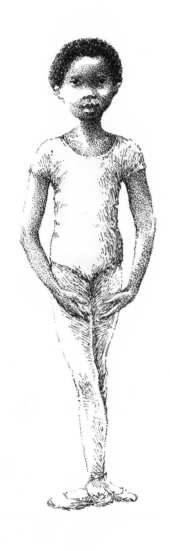

third　　　　　　　　　*fourth*　　　*and*

fifth

I wiggle.
Madeleine sees me
and giggles.

We do portes des bras.
I bend forward and try to touch
my nose to my knees.

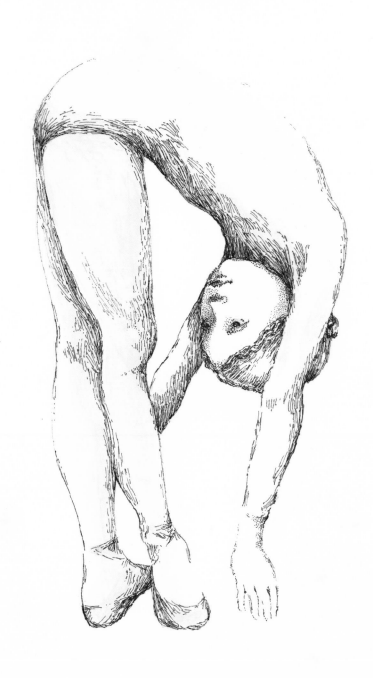

I bend back as far as I can.

The best part of class is
when we leap across the floor.
Charlie jumps the highest.

*At the end of class
we thank Mr. Lucien
with a révérence.*

We go to the
dressing room
and put on
our street clothes.

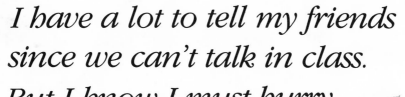

I have a lot to tell my friends since we can't talk in class. But I know I must hurry.

My father is waiting for me.